'IT'S AN
IMPR
CITY, BOLOGNA
– LIKE ONE YOU
MIGHT WALK
THROUGH AFTER
YOU HAVE DIED.'

JOHN BERGER
Born 1926, London, UK
Died 2017, Paris, France

First published in 2007.

BERGER IN PENGUIN MODERN CLASSICS
Understanding a Photograph
Ways of Seeing

JOHN BERGER

The Red Tenda of Bologna

PENGUIN BOOKS

PENGUIN CLASSICS

UK | USA | Canada | Ireland | Australia
India | New Zealand | South Africa

Penguin Books is part of the Penguin Random House group
of companies whose addresses can be found at
global.penguinrandomhouse.com.

Penguin
Random House
UK

First published by Drawbridge Books 2007
This edition first published 2018

012

Set in 10.25/12.75 pt Dante MT Std
Typeset by Jouve (UK), Milton Keynes
Printed and bound in Great Britain by Clays Ltd, Elcograf S.p.A.

ISBN: 978-0-241-33901-5

www.greenpenguin.co.uk

*Title refers to the red
linen awnings of the
city arcades/porticoes +
shops
cf P22*

The Red Tenda of Bologna

I should begin with how I loved him, in what manner, to what degree, with what kind of incomprehension.

Edgar was my father's eldest brother, born in the 80s of the nineteenth century at the time when Queen Victoria became Empress of India. When first he came to live with us, I was about ten years old and he was in his mid-fifties. Yet I thought of him as ageless. Not unchanging, certainly not immortal, but ageless because unanchored in any period, past or future. And so, as a kid, I could love him as an equal. Which I did.

According to the standards by which I was being brought up, he was a failure. He was hard-up for money, unmarried, unprepossessing, apparently without ambition. He ran a very modest employment agency in South Croydon. His principal passion was writing (and receiving) letters. He wrote to pen-pals, distant members of the family, strangers, and people he had once encountered on his travels. On his dressing table there was always a book of stamps. What he knew or surmised about the world fascinated me. And as an adolescent I loved his alternative vision, his shabby and royal intransigence.

He and I seldom embraced or touched one another, our most intimate contact was made through gifts. During three decades our gifts conformed to the same tacit, unwritten law: any gift had to be small, unusual and addressed to a particular appetite known to exist in the other.

Here is a random list of some of the gifts we exchanged.

A knife for opening envelopes
A packet of Breton galette
A map of Iceland
A pair of motorbike goggles
A paperback edition of Spinoza's *Ethics*
One and a half dozen Whitstable oysters
A biography of Dickens
A matchbox full of Egyptian sand
A bottle of Tequila, the eau de vie of the desert from Mexico

And (when he was in hospital dying) a flamboyant wide silk necktie, which I tied around the collar of his striped flannel pyjama jacket, laughing so as not to howl. He too knew why I was laughing.

I also loved him for his imperturbability. He believed in general and in principle that the best was to come. A belief hard to sustain during the twentieth century, if one didn't close one's eyes. And he carried with him everywhere three pairs of spectacles – each pair with different lenses. He examined everything. He died in 1972.

Was he the most compliant man I've ever met, or the most persistent and independent? Perhaps he was both. He was never where you expected him to be.

He practised Pelmanism and Esperanto and was a pacifist. He got around on a staid, upright bicycle with a luggage rack behind, on to which he strapped books which he was exchanging or bringing home from the Public Library in East Croydon. He had three tickets from this library so that at any given moment, he could take out at least a dozen books.

Before mounting his bike he attached a pair of bicycle clips to his legs and they gathered in his trousers just above his ankles. Like this he had a slightly Indian look, although the skin of his body was pale, and for a man, particularly soft – reminiscent of what the French call *le pain au lait*. He didn't possess a driving license, although for two years when he was thirty he had driven ambulances on the Western Front during the First World War.

Whenever I stood beside him – in the figurative or physical sense – I felt reassured. Time will tell, he used to say, and he said this in such a way that I assumed time would tell what we'd both be finally glad to hear.

Beside letter-writing his other passion was travelling. At that time many people travelled, but tourism as such did not yet exist. Travellers, rich or modest, planned their own journeys. He was a modest and persistent traveller. He believed travel broadened the mind. One of the many biographies I remember him reading was one of Thomas Cook who founded the first travel agency. Another was of Berlioz whose music, according to my uncle, was, *par excellence*, the music of travel. *Bien sûr*. He smiled with a kind of pride when he used French phrases and – less frequently – Italian ones.

After an early supper in our dining room he used to go upstairs and read in his very small bedroom, often until the small hours of the morning. The room was less than double the size of a wagon-lit cabin. In it was a radio and a typewriter, on which he typed out with two fingers his letters and thoughts. Most evenings as a boy and young adolescent I went to say goodnight to him, and I often had the impression there were at least three of us in the room with the single upright chair (I always sat on the bed when we were discussing together.) The third person was either the writer of the book he was reading or one of his favourite characters in the book. It was in this cramped room that I learnt how printed words when read can summon up a physical presence.

Much of what my Uncle read was related to the next journey he was planning or the one he had just made. The years passed and he travelled to Iceland, Norway, Russia, Denmark, India. (Maybe I'm exaggerating. Maybe one or two of these journeys were only planned in low-voiced conversations between us when we met in his South Croydon office.) He certainly did go to Egypt, Greenland and Italy.

He went south to study history and north (which he preferred) to be at home with nature.

In Italy he discovered two cousins of ours who were music teachers in Rome. Before visiting Florence he read Burckhardt's *Renaissance* and spent weeks planning exactly what he wanted to see each day and in what order. Plan your work and work your plan. Later he became fascinated by the city of Bologna.

By this time I was at art school and so I mentioned to him that Bologna was the city of Morandi. And no sooner had I said this, than I saw in a flash that he and Morandi could well put on and wear each other's shoes without either of them noticing the difference! Neither of them were married: both of them had lived at various times with a spinster sister. Their noses and mouths had the same expression of seeking an intimacy that is not carnal. The two of them liked solitary walks and both were continually curious about what they saw as they walked. The difference between them was that Morandi was an obsessional, great artist and my Uncle, who was no artist, was a passionate letter writer.

To have said any of this would have been an impertinence, and so I simply repeated several times that he should look at Morandi's paintings when he went to Bologna.

He's a very quiet man Morandi, my Uncle told me on his return.

What do you mean? He's dead. He died last year.

I know. I only saw his pictures of pots and shells and flowers. Very careful and very quiet. He could have been an architect too, wouldn't you say?

Yes, an architect.

Or a tailor!

Yes, a tailor. Did you like the city?

It's red, I've never seen a red like Bologna's. Ah! If we knew the secret of that red . . . It's a city to return to, *la proxima volta*.

In the Piazza Maggiore some steps lead up to the east face of the Basilica of St Petronius, which, like many of Bologna's historic buildings is constructed in brick. For centuries people have sat on these steps to watch what's happening in the square and to notice the minute differences between yesterday and today. I'm sitting on these steps.

No traffic except bicycles. I notice that some people crossing the square, when they are more or less at its centre, pause and lean their backs against an invisible wall of an invisible tower of air, which reaches towards the sky, and there they glance upwards to check the clouds or the sky's emptiness. In conversations about tomorrow's weather opinions here continually differ.

Five teenagers are demonstrating their talents with a football, imagining a stadium. An elderly woman, to her evident surprise, meets a five-year-old girl whom she recognizes and who appears to be here alone.

Probably they live in the same district, a bus ride from the centre, a district of worker's flats like San Donato. The woman buys the girl a helium balloon from a street vendor. The balloon has the body of a tiger, with black and yellow stripes. It slinks along wafting on high above the girl's head.

A man in his fifties carrying two plastic bags – he has been shopping for his groceries – puts them down, stoops towards me and asks me whether I have a cigarette. I take out a packet and offer him several. He has the eyes of a man more used to reading print, than looking at buildings. Only one! he insists. His canvas shoes are frayed and dusty. He uses his own lighter to light the cigarette.

At the University, ten minutes walk away to the right of where I'm facing – sixty thousand students study today. In medieval times the first secular university in Europe was established here.

The girl, with her tiger, walks towards the shop windows of the Pavaglione. Her steps are as feline as the animal above her. Even life-size tigers look weightless when walking. Way behind the tiger stand two towers, the taller of the two, built in the twelfth century, is almost one hundred metres high. During the Renaissance there were many such towers in the city – each one built by a rivalling mercantile family to demonstrate its wealth and power. One by one they collapsed and within a century you could count on one hand those that remained. After the city was annexed by Rome in the sixteenth century the population suffered from poverty and pestilence. No wages, no work, no outlets. In the last decades of the nineteenth century, thanks to Marconi, the radio, and to light precision engineering, it began to prosper again, and then became a capital of skilled labour.

The girl with her floating tiger is so enchanted that, as she looks up smiling, I imagine her listening to some bars of music. It's an improbable city, Bologna – like one you might walk through after you have died.

I leave the piazza and wander east towards the university. There are continuous arcades on both sides of the street. People here argue not only about tomorrow's weather, but about how many kilometres of arcades there are crossing the city.

The tradition of the 'porticoes', as the arcades were called, began in the early Middle Ages. Each mansion had before its door a small plot of land which gave on to the street. A number of householders had the idea of roofing over their plots. Like this they could accommodate unforeseen travellers, allow extra servants to sleep overnight, or rent accommodation to poor students from the university. At the same time the public walked from portico to portico, benefiting from the shelter, and leaving the street proper open for wagons, horses and animals. With the passing of time the city persuaded its rich house owners to take a pride in what they were offering the street, whilst imposing a certain standardization. Thus finally the porticoes became arcades.

For those living here, the arcades are a kind of personal agenda, made of stone, brick and cobbles. You can visit your creditors, your secret love, your sworn enemy, your favourite coffee shop, your mother, your dentist, your local office of unemployment, your oldest friend, or a bench where you regularly sit down utterly alone, adjusting the elastoplast you've put over a sore wart on your index finger – you can keep all these rendezvous without ever being exposed to the sky. And what difference does this make to the facts of your life? None. Yet under the arcades the echoes of those facts sound different. And in the evening Pleasure and Desolation take their evening stroll along the arcades and walk hand in hand.

All the windows I pass have awnings and all of them are of the same colour. Red. Many are faded, a few are new, but they are old and young versions of the same colour. Each fits its window exactly on the inside, and its angle is adjustable according to the amount of light desired indoors. They are called *tende*. The red is not a clay red, it's not terracotta, it's a dye red. On the other side of it are bodies and their secrets, which on the other side are not secrets.

I want to buy a length of this red *tende* linen. I'm not sure what I'll do with it. Maybe I only need it to make this portrait. Anyway I'll be able to feel it, scrumble it up, smooth it out, hold it against the sunlight, hang it, fold it, dream of what's on the other side.

I enquire about a possible shop.

Try Pasquinis, a woman tells me, near the Neptune fountain.

On my way there, in a corner of what was once long ago a pottery market, I pass a long high wall with several thousand black and white photographs, behind glass, displayed on it. Portraits of men and some women, with their names and their dates of birth and death printed across the bottom of their chests, where one might listen to their hearts if one had a stethoscope. They are arranged in alphabetical order. Mid-twentieth century. How many foresaw their portraits being placed along with thousands of other martyrs, side by side, row above row, on a public wall in the city centre? More than we might guess. In alphabetical order they knew what was at stake: in this area of Italy one out of every four anti-fascist Partisans was to lose her or his life.

I read some of their names, hearing them spoken out loud. Their faces look confident, most of them, and with the confidence there is pain. Looking at them I vaguely remember something written by Pasolini. And now, whilst writing, I have found the lines I wanted to remember:

> . . . The light
> of the future doesn't cease for even an instant
> to wound us: it is here to
> brand us in all our daily deeds
> with anxiety even in the confidence
> that gives us life . . .

After 1945 and free elections, Bologna became a communist city. And the City Council remained Communist, election following election, during fifty years. It was here that Management was obliged to accept Workers Control committees in the running of their factories. Another consequence (so easy to forget how political practice often operates like a loom, weaving in two directions, the expected and the unexpected) was that Bologna became the best conserved city in Italy, famous for its small luxuries, refinements and calm – and Europe's favourite host-city for Trade Fairs. (Sports Installations, Fashion Knitwear, Agricultural machinery, Children's Books, etc.)

The Pasquinis shop is on a corner. From the street you see nothing except the announcement: *Tessuti lino, cotone e lana, tendaggi*. Inside it looks as though nothing has changed for fifty years. Maybe some of the textiles on sale are 75% acrylic, but you wouldn't guess it.

There are three high counters, and between and behind them are hundreds of bolts of coloured fabrics, stacked up horizontally from the floor so that they make a wall. You think of a log stockade. A corral for colours.

Behind each counter a man stands in his shirt sleeves, wearing a wide leather belt with a pair of large scissors, a metre rod and a ruler stuck into it. The counters are high so that when one of these men unrolls a bolt of cloth, and, if the customer approves, cuts it with his scissors, he can work standing up, without bending.

There are two women before me. One is touching the velvet, over which she's hesitating, as if it were her daughter's just washed hair. The other is counting out loud her steps as she strides across the floorboards, calculating how many metres of a floral calico she will need.

At the end of the shop, near the entrance door, there's a high podium with a stool, table and cash-till placed on it. Seated on the stool the shop owner oversees every operation taking place. At the moment he's reading his newspaper.

The light, like the quiet, is diffused, muted, as if all the rolls of cloth had given off, over the years, a very fine, unidentifiable white cotton dust – the same dust that settled on the objects painted by Morandi, who surely knew this shop.

When my turn comes, I explain to the young assistant what I want. Like his two companions he has the air of a rancher rather than a draper. To extract the 2 metre bolt of red linen he shifts with great dexterity several others. Then he places the bolt on the counter and with a flourish unrolls about a metre. I finger the cloth.

It's a heavy linen, he says.

How much a metre? I ask.

19 euros.

OK. Give me, please, 3 metres.

He takes scissors and rod from his belt, looks at me again to check (mistakes can't be corrected), I nod, and he cuts. Folding the length I've bought four times, he slips it into a bag, writes out the bill with a pencil, also attached by a string to his belt, and nods in the direction of the podium.

I pick up the purchase, take out three 20 euro notes from my wallet and go to pay, holding the notes up high, above my head. The owner leans forward and down to take them from me, and our eyes meet. I recognize him. He pretends not to recognize me. His conspiratorial expression is familiar. The last time he put it on was when I had given him his tie and was saying goodbye to him in the hospital. Behind his bifocal glasses the swiftest flicker of one eye (his left) says: I'll see you round the corner – when the time comes.

I leave the shop without a word, return to the steps in the Piazza Maggiore, and there I look at what I've acquired and compare it to the awnings I can see in the top floor windows, surrounding the square.

Time will tell.

I turn things over in my mind. Then I fold the cloth another time, place it on the step beside me, and stretch myself out to lie along the step with my head on it, as if it were a pillow, eyes shut.

We made three voyages together, before I was fourteen years old. One to Normandy, another to Brittany and the third to Belgium and Luxembourg. When we arrived in a town – be it Ghent or Rouen or Carnac – after we found the hotel, booked by him in advance, we had a special procedure. I might say ritual – except that it was so discreet.

We had something light to eat – perhaps a small glass of white wine, and then we followed, street-name by street-name, a trail he had already prepared. Along it were surprises, for me total surprises, for him anticipated ones. Canals like streets. A gallows. A shop window with a display of white lace as fine as the stars in the furthest galaxy.

Sometimes the trail called for a taxi to take us cross-country. To cheer the Tour de France as the riders came in at the finish of the day's stint. To watch a fisherman's boat leaving at night a quayside, an oil lamp on its mast, flame flickering and never going out. To search for a megalith one could lie on – like I'm now lying on this step in the Piazza Maggiore.

All these finds which we came upon together, were as secret as wrapped presents. In fact more secret, for, once unwrapped they still remained secrets. He would put his finger with the wart on it to his lips, as a sign to remind me not to tell, to keep it to myself.

Even at that early age I sensed this was something more than a childish game. He had learnt how persistently many people need to look away from, to neutralize, what surrounds them. And one of the frequent devices they use to achieve this is to insist that everything is bound to be ordinary. The advantage of the untold is that it cannot be dismissed as ordinary. God is the unsaid, he murmured to me one evening in St Malo, drinking, before bed, a glass of Benedictine.

In the Via Caprarie we are going to find a kilo of *passatelli* in a paper bag, that looks as if it was made to hold truffles. After Easter, during the summer heat, the Bolognese stop eating lasagne and tagliatelle which are too heavy, and move on to *passatelli*, a pasta in brodo. You want the list of ingredients? 400gr. white bread crumbs, 240 gr. Parmesan cheese, 1 teaspoon of flour, 6 eggs, 1 small nutmeg, 50 gr. butter?

Teaspoons fascinated him, and on his travels he collected them. He had half a dozen teaspoons from Dublin which he kept in a flat box, like a box for war medals. Inside it the spoons lay on a dark blue velvet.

In the Via Marsala we'll eat the best mortadella in the world. Mortadella was invented here at the beginning of the 17th century. Its name comes from the fact that it is seasoned with myrtle berries. When it's good, it's eaten in chunks, not thin slices. With it, drink a white wine from Alto Adige. He raises his glass to touch mine.

Now some coffee? A merchant in the Via Porta Nuova. Here, as you see, the coffees are listed with the year of their harvesting, like wines. There are good years and poor ones. Time will tell. Coffees from all over the world, Brasil sul de Minas. Java Wib. India Parchment. Let's go straight to the best. Blue Mountain from Jamaica. When they receive a new delivery of this coffee, they put it, each night, in the safe along with the bank notes! After drinking it, the taste stays in the mouth for fifty minutes. It keeps the whole brain company.

Lying on the step I keep my eyes shut.

When you can taste it no more in your mouth, go to the church of Santa Maria della Vita.

I open my eyes to look up into the empty sky above the Piazza. I already know the church; there's a Compianto there.

A group of life-size figures made in terracotta. Fifteenth century. Christ lies dead on the ground and standing around him are Joseph of Arimathea, the rich man who bought the tomb so Jesus could be buried, Mary the mother of the apostles John and James, Mary the mother of Jesus, John the storyteller and evangelist, the Mary who was Jesus' aunt and Mary Magdalene. The sculptor is Nicolo dell'Arca who worked most of his life for the city of Bologna.

The two men in the group are calm, the four Marys are caught in a hurricane of grief. The vortex of the hurricane is Mary Magdalene. What the wind does to her clothes, the way it tears at them as she rushes forward, is the same as what her grief has done to her mouth and throat.

Yet is grief the right word? Her grief has become her own determination. Nothing will stop her.

The night after next she will be alone in the same place. The tomb will be open. Christ's body will have disappeared. Only the shroud and head cloth will remain. And she will ask the gardener where he has placed the crucified body so she may find it and tend it. And the gardener will look at her and she will instantly recognize him, and he will say: Do not touch me. And for the first time she'll believe he means it. Tell my disciples I have gone to my Father . . .

There are a few figures in art who have ended up in the wrong setting. In a painting by Velasquez there's a Madrid stone-mason, exemplary for his care and patience, who has ended up as Mars the god of war! In this compianto over the dead Christ, Mary Magdalene ends up representing every martyr – Lucy, Teresa, Cecilia, Catherine, Ursula.

She is intrepid, and in face of her nothing is mitigated.

When I arrive at the church, there is nobody else. I'm alone and I hang the *tenda*, folded as it was four times over itself on the counter, on the wrought iron railing which surrounds the Compianto group at the level of my knees.

There I wait. It crosses my mind that a *tenda*, as well as being a blind for keeping sunlight out, may also be one for keeping grief in, and for cultivating determination.

After some time, I leave the church of Santa Maria della Vita. The hurricane it contains never blows itself out. Outside the evening is peaceful. People are discussing tomorrow's weather. I enter the Pavaglione shopping centre, for I have a premonition. There is a certain place where two arcades cross under a dome. In the corners of this space are tall pilasters. Pigeons often fly through there. The sparrows don't come because there are no tables with people eating. It's a place of passage. Perhaps when the Pavaglione was used, as an indoor food market, it was the quietest place. Anyway there's an acoustic phenomenon. Which might be called 'the whispering shout.'

If you stand against a particular pilaster and look diagonally across the octagon to the corresponding one on the other side, and if somebody happens to be standing there, you can talk to them, and they can talk to you, and your voices will be very distinct and loud, however many people are passing between you, and nobody else will hear your words. The idea of a secret is stood on its head. To share a secret here you move far apart, the words resound in public, and only the two of you hear them.

My premonition is that if I wait by one of the pilasters in question, he may come.

I wait for what seems a long while. It's not that with age I have become more patient. I'm as impatient as I was when I was eleven; it's simply that I believe in time less. A dog comes up to me wagging its tail. Dogs in Bologna are rare. The dog's mistress scolds it, frowns at me and walks on, remembering, and at the same time fatally forgetting, her youth.

Suddenly he's there. He's perspiring. He has no jacket. His hands are gently clasped behind his back. He knows about the invisible acoustic telephone. He speaks with the quiet confidence of somebody who, apparently talking to himself, knows he will be heard.

Don't forget, martyrs are ordinary people, they are never the powerful. Afterwards, a little power may accrue because of the example they've set. An example sustaining thousands of little hopes. Little hopes like the pursuit of little pleasures.

He mops his brow.

It's only under this dome in the Pavaglione that we can talk of such paradoxes. Who would ever dream of putting martyrs and Blue Mountain coffee side by side? Yet they are closer than the moralists pretend, very close.

He peers through his glasses at me.

Martyrs are enviable. They're to be pitied for the pain they suffer, for at one moment it is pain, very harsh pain. Yet they are also enviable.

I nod.

They have learnt how to be touched – that is the special gift of martyrs, warriors never learn it.

One of the buttons of his white shirt is undone and he does it up with his right hand without glancing at it, whilst continuing his whispering.

They know before they die that their life has served for something. Many would envy that.

Even if the cause they believe in was lost? I ask.

I believe so, yes. Anyway I'm not sure history has winners and losers any more than justice does. Martyrs die to have a home everywhere. That's why they are honoured by the poor. When they are honoured in palaces, the martyrs, they revolt and disappear – leaving behind only their relics.

He takes off his spectacles and wipes them on a handkerchief he takes from the breast pocket of his shirt.

Surely the little pleasures, I reply, belong not to death but to life.

So does martyrdom. He says this as if he wants me to hear every letter of the words. It's the coincidence of opposites. Amongst martyrs, and in the pursuit of little refined pleasures, there is something of the same defiance, and of the same modesty. At a different level naturally. But the coincidence remains. Both defy the cruelties of life.

You make me think of a painting by Caravaggio.

What of?

The martyrdom of St Ursula.

His laughter fills the dome, and nobody apart from me hears it. People are walking faster before the shops shut.

Ursula is rumour from beginning to end. He opens both palms in a gesture of humility and resignation. Street gossip. The woman lived in the 3rd century and her story was only told in the 9th. Some respect for the facts. At the end of the 4th century, a basilisk near Cologne was being repaired and the masons discovered a mass grave, all of them women, said to be virgins. They carved an inscription without citing a name or date. Four centuries pass, and along comes a storyteller. This storyteller finds the name of Ursula on a grave somewhere else. The grave of a child, who had died aged eight. Misreading the Roman numerals, he further proposes that Ursula, who has become overnight the daughter of the King of England, was accompanied on a pilgrimage by eleven thousand other virgins! There were understandably not enough ships for them to cross the Channel. So the ships had to be built. Whilst waiting, the women themselves learnt to sail and to become intrepid sailors. They crossed the Channel together, they sailed up the Rhine as far as Basel, and from there they walked over the Alps to Rome.

He shakes his head and waits, and we both watch the people passing through the arcade.

It was on their return journey that disaster befell them. Not far from Cologne they fell into the hands of Attila and his thugs and all of them who resisted were massacred.

He passes his thumb slowly along his lower lip.

There have always been rumours. They're inevitable. They help us to come to terms with what is forcefully denied and may be true.

He dabs at his mouth with his handkerchief. When he takes it away, his mouth is smiling.

So be it. Bologna! Bologna! Near the Porta S. Vitale there's a bar called the Bocca d'Oro, where they serve, if you insist on the one made by the capo's mother, the best *limoncello* you've ever tasted. It promises everything.

Only the pilaster now. He's gone. In my ears only the sounds of the city.